This book belongs to:

Camilla the Cupcake Fairy

Magic Sprinkles

Other books in the series:

Magic Wand

Best Friends

Tea Party

Copyright © 2011 make believe ideas ltd.
The Wilderness, Berkhamsted, Hertfordshire, HP4 2AZ, UK.
565 Royal Parkway, Nashville, TN 37214, USA.

Reading together

This book is designed to be fun for children who are just starting to read on their own. They will enjoy and benefit from some time discussing the story with an adult. Encourage them to pause and talk about what is happening in the pictures. Help them to spot familiar words and sound out the letters in harder words. Look at the following ways you can help your child take those first steps in reading:

Look at rhymes

The sentences in this book are written with simple rhymes. Encourage your child to recognize the rhyming words. Try asking the following questions:

- What does this word say?

- Can you find a word that rhymes with it?

- Look at the ending of two rhyming words – are they spelled the same? For example, "tree" and "see."

Test understanding

It is one thing to understand one word at a time, but it is important to make sure your child can understand the story as a whole!

Ask your child questions as you read the story, for example:

- Did Camilla use her sprinkles to make cupcakes?

- Where did Camilla find the sprinkles?

- Did the sprinkles make Camilla and her friends happy?

- Play "find the obvious mistake." Read the text as your child looks at the words with you, but make an obvious mistake to see if he or she catches it. Ask your child to correct you and provide the right word.

Activity section

A "Ready to tell" section at the end of the book encourages children to remember what happened in the story and then retell it. A dictionary page helps children to increase their vocabulary, and a useful word page reinforces their knowledge of the most common words. There is also a practical activity inspired by the story and a "Camilla and her friends" section where children can learn about all of Camilla the Cupcake Fairy's friends!

When Camilla found some sprinkles
under the cupcake tree,
she put them in her pocket,
hoping no one else would see.

She thought some fancy frosting
was what they would make,

but soon found out,
without a doubt,
she'd made a big mistake!

Camilla made some cupcakes
and, sitting in her chair,
she took the magic sprinkles
and threw them in the air!

They flew right out the window,
which was really not her plan.

They landed by her fairy friends and the magic soon began!

Cranberry turned bright purple
with creamy swirls on top.

His fish turned into
chocolate drops —
the magic would not stop!

Miss Sprinkle's van began to shrink, as the magic struck some more.

She got so squished,
she turned bright pink,
and her head got very sore!

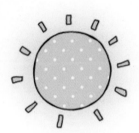

Maya's hair became green frosting, whipped high just like ice cream.

Camilla thought,
"It's all my fault!"
and then began to scream!

She woke with a start
and soon took heart.
It was really just a dream!

Camilla felt much better,
so happy she nearly burst!
But she learned
that it's wrong to take things
without asking nicely first!

Ready to tell

Can you remember what happened in the story? Look at each picture and then try retelling the story.

Camilla's fairy dictionary

mistake When you make a mistake, you do something wrong.

shrink To shrink is to become smaller in size.

sore When something is sore, it hurts.

burst If you burst a balloon, it suddenly breaks or pops.

whipped When cream is whipped, it is shaken or stirred until it is thick and fluffy.

Camilla's useful words

Here are some key words used in context. Make simple sentences for the other words in the border.

Camilla found some sprinkles **under** the cupcake tree.

She **thought** she could make some frosting for the cupcakes.

The sprinkles flew **away**.

The sprinkles caused a lot **of** trouble.

Luckily it **was** all a dream.

Camilla and her friends

Camilla loves making cupcakes and using her wand to make magical toppings! She sometimes gets a little confused, but she never gives up and is a true friend to the other cupcake fairies.

Connie loves art and crafts. She's always drawing, painting, or gluing. Most of all, she loves making gifts for her friends.

Molly is kind, thoughtful, and a bit of a dreamer. She's always coming up with new things to do and try. Sometimes they are a little crazy!

Maya is super-smart. She's always reading recipe books and inventing new cakes and toppings. Her favorite day of the year is Cupcake Day when all the fairies have a bake-off!

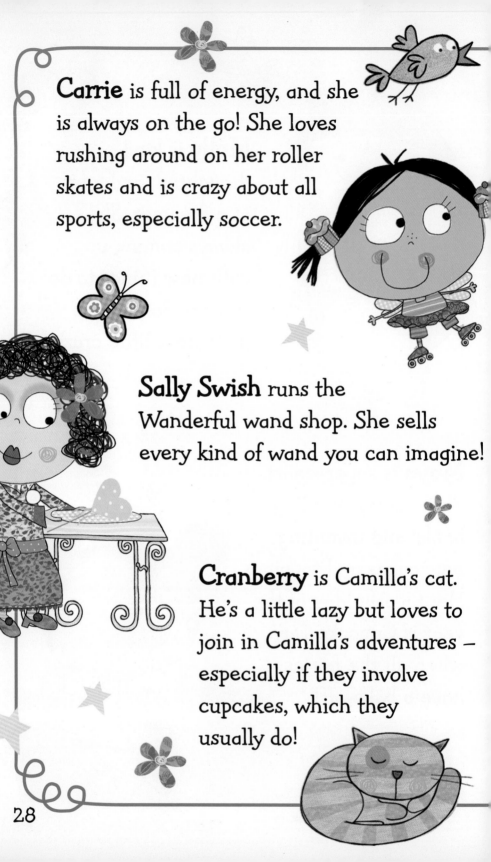

Carrie is full of energy, and she is always on the go! She loves rushing around on her roller skates and is crazy about all sports, especially soccer.

Sally Swish runs the Wanderful wand shop. She sells every kind of wand you can imagine!

Cranberry is Camilla's cat. He's a little lazy but loves to join in Camilla's adventures – especially if they involve cupcakes, which they usually do!

Miss Sprinkles
is the cupcake fairies'
teacher. She is very kind and wise and will
always help the fairies if they have a problem.

Sandy Swirls has a very
important job: delivering the
fairy mail! On a cupcake fairy's
fifth birthday, Sandy
delivers their very
first magic wand.

Make a cupcake crown

You will need:

1 sheet of white cardboard
marker pens
scissors
1 old headband
sticky tape
glue
glitter and beads
silver foil

Camilla loves her cupcake crown – now you can make one yourself!

What to do:

1. On your sheet of cardboard, draw a rectangle that will be long enough to fit around the width of your headband. Ask a grown-up to help you cut it out and then loop it around the headband, taping it so that it holds tightly in place.

2. Next, draw a cupcake on the rest of your piece of cardboard. You can decorate it however you like! Try adding glitter and gluing silver foil to it.

3. Ask a grown-up to help you cut the cupcake out. Then put some glue on the back. Stick the cupcake to the front of the cardboard on the headband, so that when you wear the headband, the cupcake will be facing forward. You could also make sure it stays in place by using sticky tape.

4. Now you should have your very own cupcake crown!

Hints and tips:

- You can make crowns in lots of different shapes; try a star or a flower!
- You could make a second cupcake and attach it to the back of your crown to cover the loop. This will make sure your crown looks lovely from both sides!

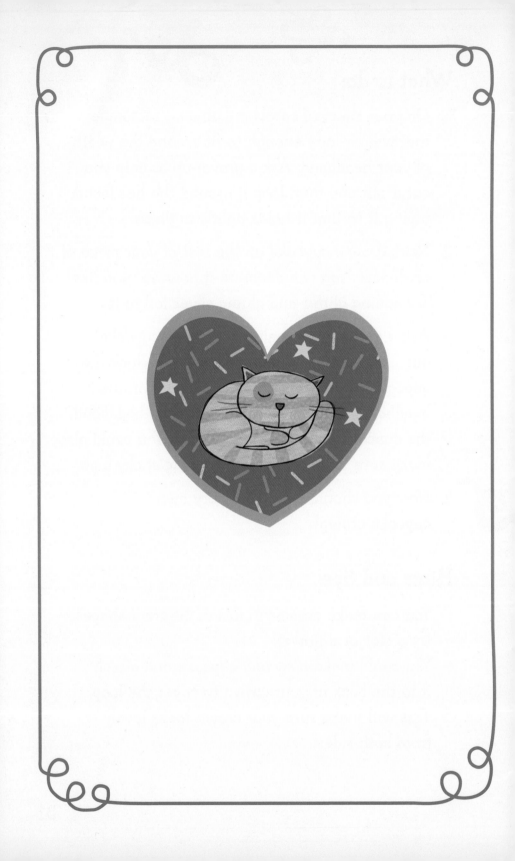